This Faber book belongs to

For my muse, who keeps me from getting too serious.
And to Sue -- for seriously everything! *J.P.*

For Florence *D.R.*

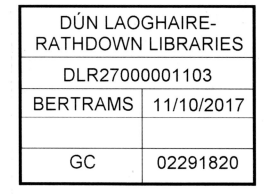

First published in the UK in 2017
by Faber and Faber Ltd,
Bloomsbury House,
74–77 Great Russell Street, London WC1B 3DA

Printed in China

Text © Jodie Parachini, 2017
Illustrations © Daniel Rieley, 2017

The right of Jodie Parachini to be identified as the Author of this Work and of Daniel Rieley to be identified as the
Illustrator of this Work have been asserted by them in accordance with the Copyright, Designs and Patent Act,
1988 (United Kingdom)

A CIP record for this book is available
from the British Library

ISBN 978–0–571–32946–5 paperback

10 9 8 7 6 5 4 3 2 1

FSC
www.fsc.org
MIX
Paper from
responsible sources
FSC® C020056

This is a SERIOUS Book

Words by Jodie Parachini
Pictures by Daniel Rieley

ff

FABER & FABER

This is a serious book.

Everything in this book is

thoughtful, proper, respectable

and, of course, *very, very* serious.

Nothing silly is allowed.

Here is a list of things not allowed
in a **serious** book:

funny faces,

backflips,

dressing up,

jumping up and down.

And **definitely** no bottom parps.

Excuse me - this means you.
Shhh!

A serious book would never have
anything **ridiculous,**
like ducky pyjamas . . .

. . . or unicycles.

Also, a serious book **must** be in black and white.

Ahem! This means you.

Wait a minute . . .

Who are *you*?

Yes, you're black and white, but you're not serious!

If you two are going to stay in this book,
you need to be serious.

Try pretending you're at a museum.

No! Not like that.

Okay, try pretending you're in a library.

No! Quiet!

sssssssssss

Who are *you*?

Go away!

This is a **serious** book!

This isn't working.

I'm sorry; you're all going to have to leave straightaway.

A serious book **isn't silly**; it explains things.

Now, where was I?

Hang on. Now there's a penguin!

I told you all to leave, not to have a parade!

PLEASE! No. More. Animals!

Monkeys?

No!

Absolutely not!

A serious book **never, ever** has monkeys.

And that's final!

Now what's going on?

Hey! Don't do that!

OK, I give up!

Do whatever you want.

Have a party!

Sing, swing, eat cake!

Dance on the ceiling.

Write your **own** book!

This is a . . .

NOT SO

serious book!

MORE FABER PICTURE BOOKS . . .

→→ FABER YOUNG SERIES ←←

Growing up
with Faber
www.faber.co.uk